PRESENTED BY

Bob
Willingham

1980

SMYTHE
GAMBRELL
LIBRARY

WESTMINSTER
SCHOOLS

D.C.L.

Doghouse
for
Sale

Doghouse for Sale

By Donna Lugg Pape

Drawings by Tom Eaton

GARRARD PUBLISHING COMPANY
CHAMPAIGN, ILLINOIS

J
Easy
Pape

Dedicated to
Jean Carol Pape

Library of Congress Cataloging in Publication Data

Pape, Donna Lugg.
    Doghouse for sale.

    (Imagination books)
    SUMMARY: Freckles the dog fixes up his house
in order to attract prospective buyers, but then has
second thoughts.

    [1. Dogs — Fiction] I. Eaton, Tom. II. Title.
PZ7.P1978Do   [E]   78-11685
ISBN 0-8116-4415-4

Doghouse for Sale

Freckles sat and looked
at his gray doghouse.

"I need
a new doghouse,"
he said,
"but I must sell
this one first."

Freckles made a sign.

DOGHOUSE

FOR

SALE

Dogs came to look
at Freckles' doghouse.

But no one
wanted to buy it.
"It needs to be painted,"
one dog said.

"Then I'll paint my house,"
said Freckles.
"I'll paint it red.
Then someone will buy it."

Freckles went to the store.
He got red paint
and a big paintbrush.

He worked hard.
Soon the doghouse
was painted red.
"There, that looks better,"
he said.

Freckles made a new sign.

RED

DOGHOUSE

FOR

SALE

Dogs came to look
at Freckles' doghouse.
But no one
wanted to buy it.

One dog said,
"Your house
needs a new bed."

"Then I'll make
a new bed
for my doghouse,"
said Freckles.
"Then someone will buy it."

He went to the store
to buy what he would need.

He worked hard.
Soon the doghouse
had a new bed.

Freckles made a new sign.

FOR SALE

RED

DOGHOUSE

WITH

NEW

BED

Dogs came to look
at Freckles' doghouse.
But no one
wanted to buy it.

One dog said,
"Your house needs a window."

"Then I'll make a window
for my doghouse,"
said Freckles.
"Then someone will buy it."

He went to the store
to buy a saw.

He worked hard.
Soon the doghouse
had a window.

Freckles made a new sign.

FOR SALE

RED

DOGHOUSE

WITH NEW BED

AND A

WINDOW

Dogs came
to look at Freckles' house.
But no one
wanted to buy it.

"Your house would look better
with some flowers
in the yard,"
one dog said.

"Then I'll plant some flowers,"
said Freckles.

Freckles went to the store.

"I want to buy some flowers,"
Freckles said.

He planted the flowers
around his doghouse.

Then he made a new sign.

FOR SALE

RED

DOGHOUSE

WITH A

NEW BED,

A WINDOW,

AND

FLOWERS

More dogs came
to look at Freckles' house.
"We like your house
very much,"
the dogs told Freckles.
"But it needs a fence
around the yard."
"A fence," said Freckles.
"That's what my house needs!"

Freckles went to the store.
"I want to buy a fence
for my doghouse,"
he said.
He bought a white fence.

Soon Freckles
had put the fence
around his doghouse.

Then he made a new sign.

FOR SALE

RED

DOGHOUSE

WITH A NEW BED,

A WINDOW,

FLOWERS,

AND A

WHITE FENCE

Dogs came
to look at the house.
"That's a fine doghouse,"
a dog told Freckles.
"I want to buy it,"
said another.

Freckles walked
around his house.
He looked
at the red paint.
He looked
at the window.
He looked
at the pretty flowers.
He looked
at the white fence.
"This is a fine doghouse,"
Freckles said.
"I don't want to sell it."

Then Freckles went
inside his house
to take a nap
in his new bed.

3